This Book Belongs To ---------------

------------------------------------

------------------------------------

------------------------------------

------------------------------------

NAME

PHONE

EMAIL

Made in the USA
Monee, IL
10 March 2021

62423217R00056